A Note to Parents

Reading books aloud and playing w
can help their children learn to read. The easy to read stories in the **My First Hello Reader! With Flash Cards** series are designed to be enjoyed together. Six activity pages and 16 flash cards in each book help reinforce phonics, sight vocabulary, reading comprehension, and facility with language. Here are some ideas to develop your youngster's reading skills:

Reading with Your Child
- Read the story aloud to your child and look at the colorful illustrations together. Talk about the characters, setting, action, and descriptions. Help your child link the story to events in his or her own life.
- Read parts of the story and invite your child to fill in the missing parts. At first, pause to let your child "read" important last words in a line. Gradually, let your child supply more and more words or phrases. Then take turns reading every other line until your child can read the book independently.

Enjoying the Activity Pages
- Treat each activity as a game to be played for fun. Allow plenty of time to play.
- Read the introductory information aloud and make sure your child understands the directions.

Using the Flash Cards
- Read the words aloud with your child. Talk about the letters and sounds and meanings.
- Match the words on the flash cards with the words in the story.
- Help your child find words that begin with the same letter and sound, words that rhyme, and words with the same ending sound.
- Challenge your child to put flash cards together to make sentences from the story and create new sentences.

Above all else, make reading time together a fun time. Show your child that reading is a pleasant and meaningful activity. Be generous with your praise and know that, as your child's first and most important teacher, you are contributing immensely to his or her command of the printed word.

—Tina Thoburn, Ed.D.
Educational Consultant

For Trina-Bug
—KH

No part of this publication may be reproduced in whole or in part, or stored in a retrieval system, or transmitted in any form or by any means, electronic, mechanical, photocopying, recording, or otherwise, without written permission of the publisher. For information regarding permission, write to Scholastic Inc., 555 Broadway, New York, NY 10012.

ISBN 0-590-25499-5
Copyright © 1996 by Nancy Hall, Inc.
All rights reserved. Published by Scholastic Inc.
CARTWHEEL BOOKS and the CARTWHEEL BOOKS logo
are registered trademarks of Scholastic Inc.
MY FIRST HELLO READER! and the MY FIRST HELLO READER! logo
are trademarks of Scholastic Inc.

12 11 10 9 8 7 6 5 4 3 2 1   6 7 8 9/9 0 1/0

Printed in the U.S.A.
First Scholastic printing, February 1996

I SEE A BUG

by Kirsten Hall
Illustrated by Eldon Doty

**My First Hello Reader!
With Flash Cards**

SCHOLASTIC INC.
Cartwheel BOOKS

New York   Toronto   London   Auckland   Sydney

I see a bug!

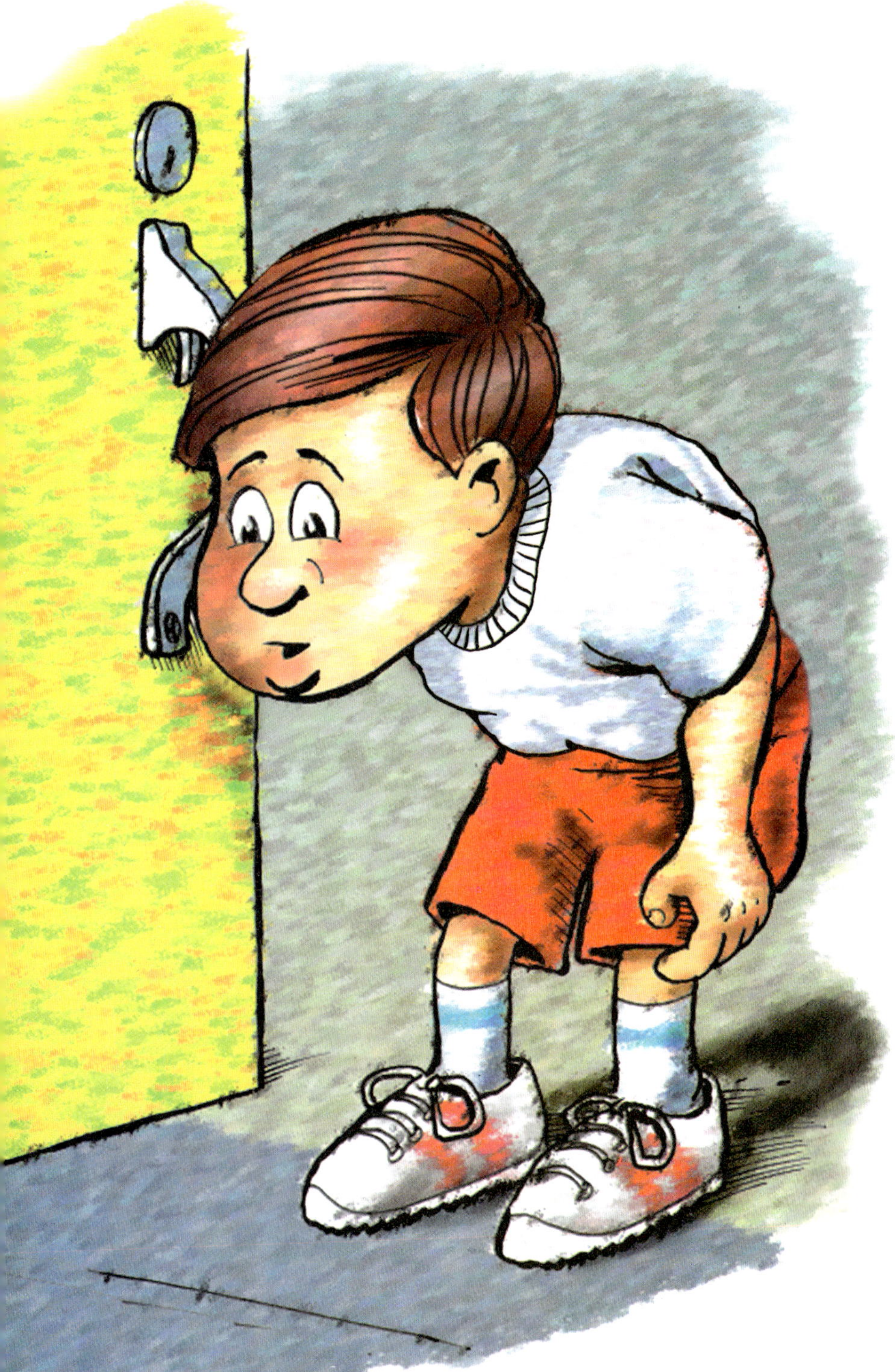

I see one more.

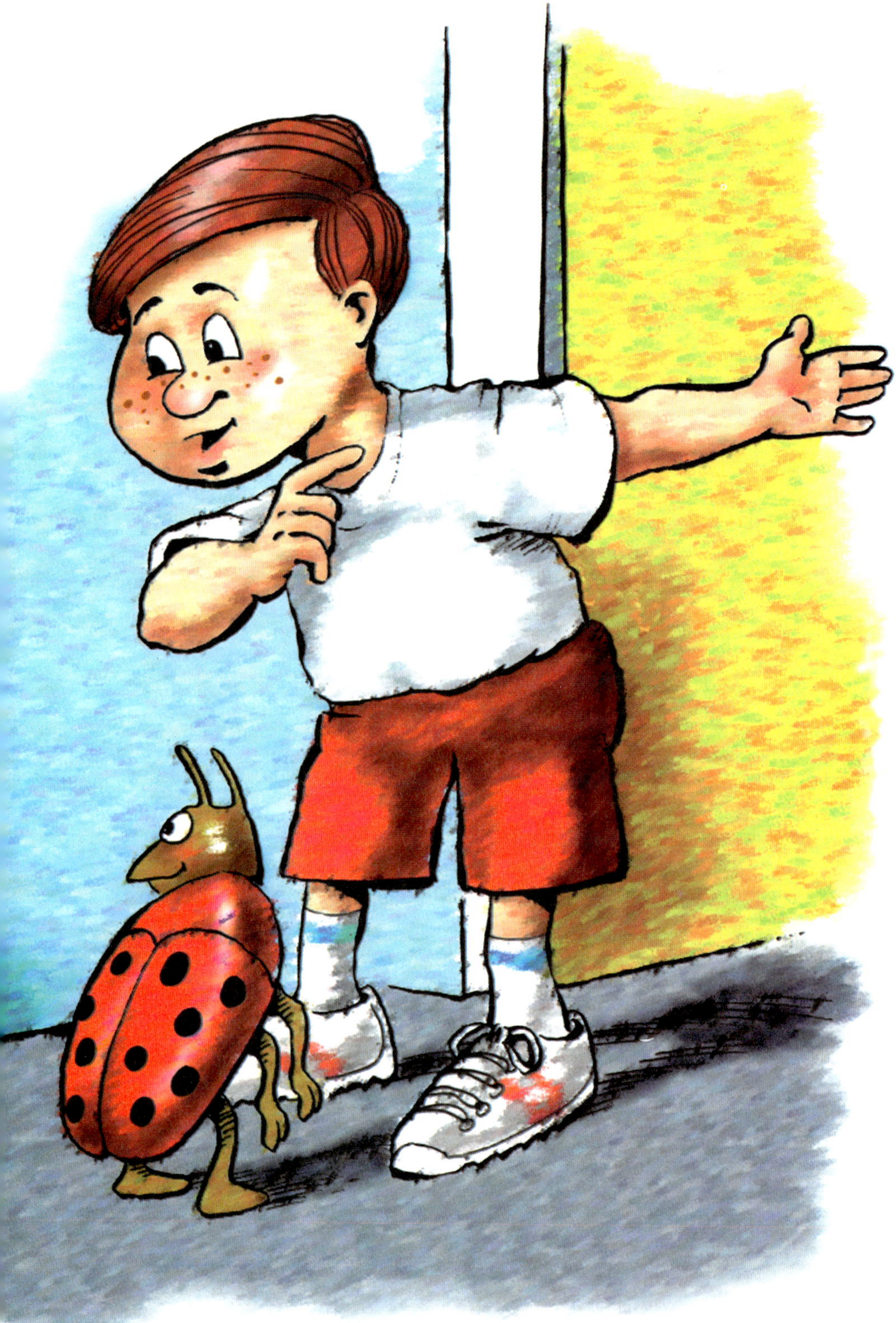

I see a third

march in my door.

March in! March in!

March in, bug four!

March right upstairs!

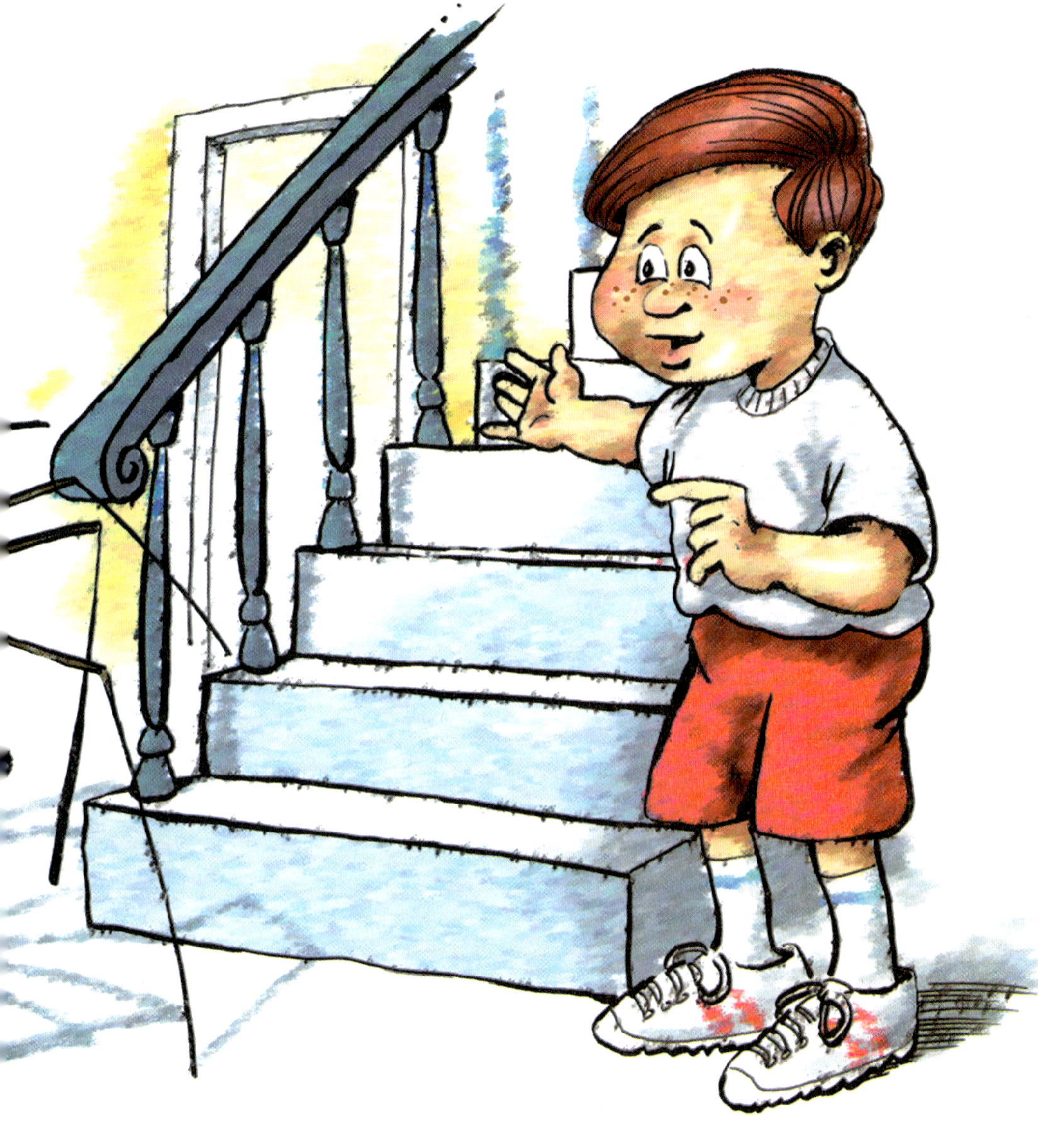

Oh no, one more?

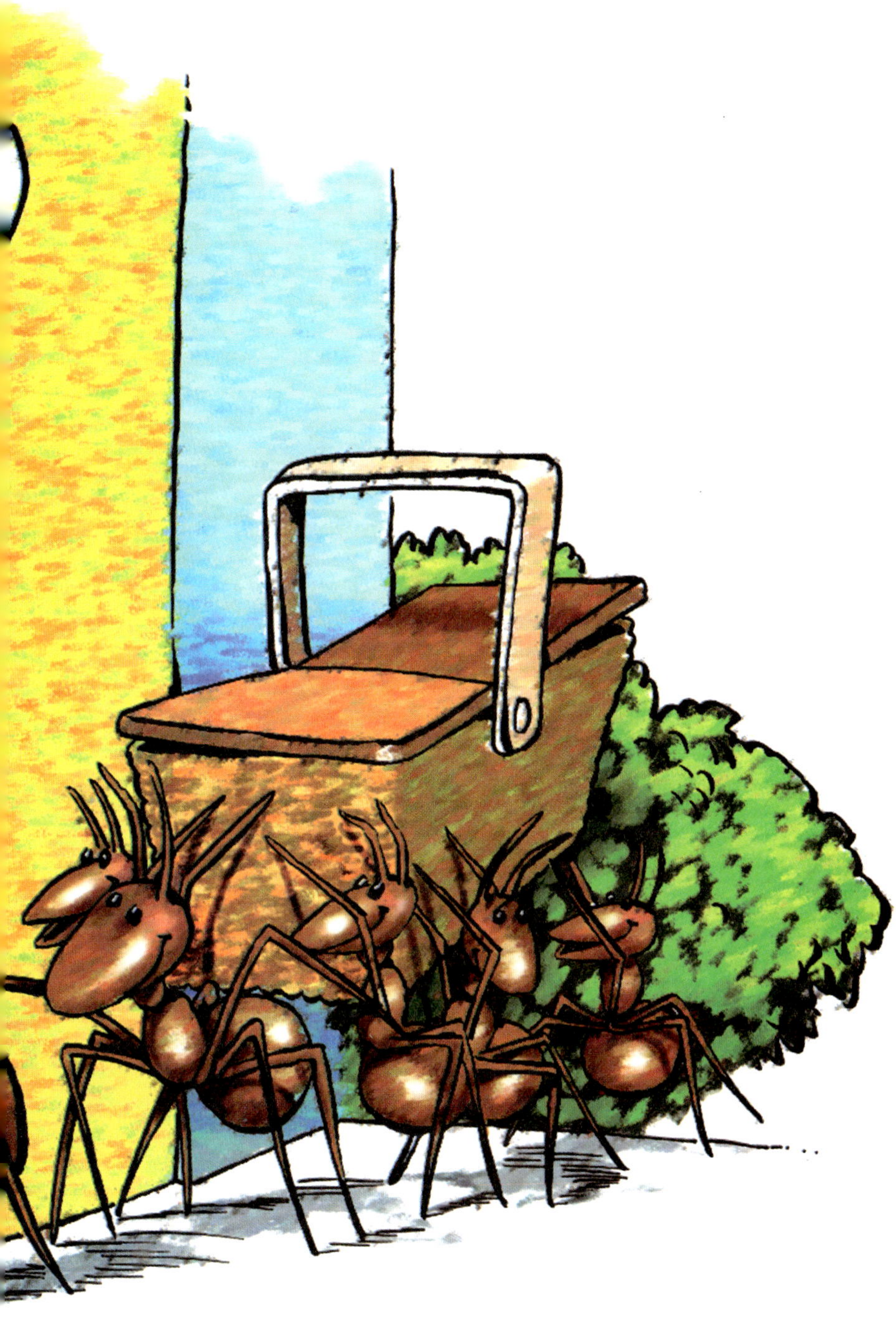

Another bug?

You brought a friend?

March in! March in!

I see no end!

No more! No more!

No, not in there!

Oh, no—you gave my mom a scare!

March out! March out!

March right outside!

Outside, where no bug has to hide!

About Face!

Here are some pictures of the boy and his mother from the story. Look at their faces and tell what you think they are feeling.

Rhyme Lines

In each line, name the pictures to make a rhyme.

I see a 🐞 on a 🟢 .

I see a 🐭 in a 🏠 .

I see a 🥄 on the 🌙 .

A Buggy Ball

The bugs are having a ball. Point to the two bugs that look the same.

To Be or Not

Look at these pictures. Point to the things that do **not** begin with the letter **B**.

Talk About It

Some people are afraid of bugs. Other people like bugs.

How do **you** feel about bugs? Why?

Bug Traffic

The bugs are driving to a party.

How many bugs are in the red car?

Which cars have **more** bugs than the red car?

Which car has the **most** bugs in it?

Answers

(*About Face!*)
    Answers will vary.

(*Rhyme Lines*)
    I see a **bug** on a **rug**.
    I see a **mouse** in a **house**.
    I see a **spoon** on the **moon**.

(*A Buggy Ball*)
    These two bugs look the same:

(*To Be or Not*)
    These do not begin with B:

(*Talk About It*)
    Answers will vary.

(*Bug Traffic*)
    There are three bugs in the red car.

These cars have more:

This car has the most: